For Becky, Nick & Graham

Library of Congress Cataloging-in-Publication Data

Ross, Christine.

The Whirlys and the west wind / Christine Ross. - 1st American ed.

p.   cm.

Summary: When Mr. and Mrs. Whirly are blown away by strong winds and remain floating in the sky for several days, their children are forced to fend for themselves.

ISBN 0-395-65379-7

[1. Winds - Fiction. 2. Family life - Fiction.] I. Title.

PZ7.R719625Wh 1993

[E] - dc20

92-39011
CIP
AC

Produced by Mandarin

Printed and bound in Hong Kong

10 9 8 7 6 5 4 3 2 1

The Whirlys and the West Wind

Christine Ross

Houghton, Mifflin Company
Boston 1993

Mr. and Mrs. Whirly and their children Flora, Jack and baby Rose lived in a house by a river.

They were a very ordinary family, who were hardly
ever surprised by anything until . . .

. . . one day the west wind blew so fiercely that it lifted
Mr. and Mrs. Whirly up into the sky.
    The children ran to save them, but it was too late.

The children turned to the emergency pages at the back of
the phone book, but there were no instructions for west wind-
made disasters.

They listened to the weather forecast. *The outlook is for strong, galeforce westerlies followed by even stronger galeforce westerlies*, it said.

It seemed their parents might be gone for quite some time.

Day after day the wind whistled and whined outside. Meanwhile, inside, things got into a muddle.

Then the muddle got into a mess . . .

And when the mess became
a maze where nothing could
be found, the children said,
"We need someone to look
after us. But who?"

Then they decided, "We'll
have to take turns looking
after ourselves."

So they did.

On Mondays and Thursdays Jack was in charge. From nine till three they all went to school.

In the evenings they did his homework and had fish and chips for supper.

On Tuesdays and Fridays
it was Flora's turn, so
they played pirates all day long.

And on Wednesdays and Sundays it was baby Rose's turn, so they made Playdough dinosaurs, read stories, ate lots of jelly sandwiches and chopped-up apple, read more stories and went to bed early.

On Saturdays they tidied up.

They kept a look-out for their mother and father with the telescope and often saw them flying across the sky — sometimes from right to left and sometimes from left to right.

Then one day everything suddenly seemed different.
The wind had dropped. By afternoon dark clouds gathered
and the rain began to fall. It rained and rained. The whole
sky seemed to be falling on to the earth.

They searched for their parents among the dark clouds but could find no sign of them. Then they noticed a strange shape floating down the swollen river. It was their mother and father! The rain had swept them out of the sky and back down the river.

Mr. and Mrs. Whirly were very happy to be back.
They were dazzled by the sparkling house and impressed by
how well Rose could read. They didn't seem to be much the
worse for wear after their strange trip.

"It was quite invigorating, really," they agreed. "Perhaps we could do it again sometime."

"No way!" said Jack.

"Well, perhaps just once," suggested Flora.

"... if you're very good," added baby Rose.